10 Fun

For 2 to 5 Year Olds

Katrina Kahler

30 years Elementary Teaching Experience

Copyright © KC Global Enterprises

Thank you for reading to your child! You are giving them the best possible start to their education.

These stories carry little messages like: being brave, telling the truth and trying your best.

I hope you and your child enjoy them.

Katrina

Table of Contents

Gus, the Grateful Fish

There were many different pets in the pet store. It was full of all kinds of animals.

Some were big, some were small, some were furry, some had feathers and some even had scales.

But when Robbie walked into the store one day, every single pet stared at him hopefully.

They were all waiting for someone to be their new owner. Each of the pets wanted a home to live in and an owner who would love them.

And each time someone walked into the store, the pets would hold their breath, hoping that this would be the perfect new owner for them.

They would smile their biggest smile and look as friendly as they could, in the hope that they would be chosen.

"I want a nice little old lady to take me home," said a ginger cat named Felix.

"Then I can snuggle up on her lap and sleep in comfort all day long. I would love that!"

"I want an active boy to take me home," said a spotted dog named Darcy.

"Then he can throw sticks and balls for me to fetch every day. I would love that!"

"I want a friendly little girl to take me home," said a cute little white mouse named Millie. "Then I can sit on her shoulder while she feeds me cheese each day. I would love that!"

"And I want a musical family to take me home," said a very pretty, yellow canary named Casper. "Then I can sing to them from my beautiful gilded cage which I can come and go from as I please. I would love that!"

"Well, I just want someone who is kind and caring," said a brightly colored rainbow fish named Gus. "Then I can swim around in my own roomy fish tank and have plenty to eat. That's what I would love!"

And each of them stared hopefully at Robbie, because the truth was that they just wanted a nice home to go to and a nice owner to love them.

They didn't really care if it were a little old lady, or an active boy or a friendly little girl or a musical family.

As long as their new owner was kind and caring, then they would feel very happy and loved. Anything was better than being cramped up in the pet store in cages and enclosures with all the other animals.

Every day there were visitors to the store and people staring at each and every one of them, but these pets hadn't been lucky enough to find an owner who would take them home.

That was until the day that Robbie walked in. "Which pet do you want, Robbie?" asked his mom as they wandered around looking in all the enclosures and cages.

"Would you like a nice ginger cat?" she asked as she stared briefly at Felix.

"No, I already have a cat!" he replied. "It would just want to sit on my lap all day and sleep, just like the cat I have now. I wouldn't like that!"

"Would you like a spotted puppy dog?" asked his dad, looking curiously at Darcy.

"No, I don't want a puppy dog!" he replied. "Then I would have to throw balls and sticks every day. I wouldn't like that!"

"What about a cute little white mouse?" asked his mom, as she stood looking at Millie.

"No, I don't want a mouse!" Robbie declared. "It would just want me to feed it all day long. I would not like that!"

Well, how about a beautiful yellow canary?" asked his dad while Casper looked on hopefully.

"No, I don't want a canary!" said Robbie furiously. "It would just want to sing all day long. I would not like that either!"

"I know," he cried, "A rainbow fish! I don't have one of those. And a fish is the perfect pet! I can watch it swim around in my fish tank and feed it fish food once each day. I think I would really like that!"

Gus smiled broadly. Finally someone had decided to take him home. Today was his lucky day. His new owner was happy to feed him each day and watch him swim around in his own roomy fish tank. His dream had finally come true.

Gus said goodbye to his friends. He would miss all the other pets in the pet store but he was very glad to be leaving. Finally he would have a home to call his own.

The pet store attendant scooped Gus up in his net and popped him into a bag full of water that was tied securely at the top. This way, Robbie could take him safely home in the car. Everything was going smoothly. Gus was sitting quietly in the plastic bag full of water that Robbie was holding on his lap, a beaming smile lighting up his face as he thought about his new home.

But then something happened. It seemed that Robbie was starting to get bored because he began shaking the bag furiously up and down. "What's he doing?" thought Gus frantically as he was being shaken to and fro.

"What's wrong with this fish?" yelled Robbie. "It's not moving!" And he shook the bag even harder.

"Just be careful, Robbie," said his mom from the front seat of the car. "I'm sure the fish will be fine once you put it into your tank at home."

"It better be!" demanded Robbie, an unsatisfied look on his face.

Gus started to worry. He hoped that Robbie was going to be happy with him. He hoped that he was going to be kind and caring and feed him fish food every day. And he hoped that he would have a lovely big tank to swim around in.

As soon as they got home, Robbie raced inside, dumped the bag with Gus still inside it on the kitchen table and ran outside to play on the new bike that his dad had bought for him that morning.

"Come back!" called Gus. "You've forgotten me! Don't you have a lovely big tank to put me into so that you can feed me fish food each day?" he cried.

But Robbie was nowhere to be seen and Gus was left alone on the kitchen table still in the plastic bag from the pet store.

"I'm sure he'll be back soon!" thought Gus hopefully, as he swam around in the little bag. "I'll just have to be patient and wait. Then I can go into my roomy new tank and Robbie can feed me fish food each day.

Just as Gus was about to take a little nap while he waited for Robbie to come back, he suddenly jumped with fright. In fact he got such a fright that his head hit the top of the bag that he was swimming around in.

Right by the open window, looking towards him and looking very scary was a huge grey and white cat.

"Hmmm!" said the cat. "Where did you come from?" he asked, a wicked grin on his hungry looking face.

Gus stared at the cat in horror. "Oh no!" he thought to himself. "Please don't eat me," he cried desperately. "I'm Gus's new pet fish. You can't eat me! He just brought me home from the pet store!"

"Is that so?" said the hungry looking cat. "But Robbie's not here right now and I'm feeling pretty hungry," he declared.

And just as Gus thought that this was the end, Robbie raced back into the house. "My fish!" he called as he grabbed the bag off the dining table and ran up the stairs to his room. "I'd almost forgotten about you!" he said, as he opened up the bag and poured Gus straight out into his tank.

Gus was swirled and tossed and turned as the water spun him around and around. When he finally got his balance and was able to look around him, he realized that he wasn't alone. Swimming around him and staring at him threateningly were about ten other fish of all different colors, shapes and sizes.

But an instant later, they all sped to the top of the tank, gobbling up the bits of food that Robbie had just dropped into the water. By this time, Gus was feeling very hungry and tried to grab some little pieces of food that were floating nearby.

But unfortunately, he wasn't quick enough. A streamlined orange swordtail zipped past him and gobbled up the flecks of food. As Gus looked around hopefully, he watched the last crumb of food being eaten by a fierce looking rainbow shark.

Gus swam sadly to a corner of the tank where he tried to hide amongst some long strands of weed. He was hungry, he was scared and he missed all his friends at the pet store. This was not the home that he had been hoping for and he didn't know what he was going to do!

Gus hid amongst the strands of weed throughout the entire night, feeling lonely and sad.

What had he gotten himself into? He had thought that Robbie was going to be kind and caring. He had thought that he would have a roomy fish tank to call his own with plenty of food to eat. But it just wasn't the case. And the fish in this tank didn't seem very friendly at all. They were all beautiful varieties of fish and they stared at him in a very unfriendly manner. He was just a rainbow fish and they didn't think that he was good enough to be in their tank.

As Gus swam quietly amongst the strands of weed, trying to keep hidden and stay out of the way of the other fish, a very beautiful goldfish swam next to him.

"Hello," she said, in a friendly voice. "My name is Gina. What's yours?"

"I'm Gus," he replied shyly. He had never seen such a beautiful fish before and had certainly never spoken to one either.

"Welcome to our tank!" she continued in her friendly way. "You don't have to be scared. The other fish seem unfriendly at first, but they're not really. They're just protective because we only get fed once a day. And another fish in the tank means less food for them."

"I see!" said Gus sadly. "This certainly isn't what I was expecting."

"You'll get used to it," said Gina. "You just have to be quick at feeding time, so that you manage to get some food for yourself! When Robbie comes to feed us next, I'll help you," she continued kindly.

Gus's spirits lifted just a little. At least he had made a friend and she was the most beautiful friend he had ever met. And she certainly seemed kind and caring. So he convinced himself to be grateful for that at least.

Each night before Robbie went to sleep he dropped a pinch of fish food into the tank. Sometimes he would drop in two pinches of food, but not often. Gradually Gus got used to life in his new home. The tank was crowded, there wasn't much to eat, but he now had the nicest, kindest, most caring friend that he had ever had. And she was definitely the most beautiful.

One day, something very unexpected happened. Robbie's cousin came to visit. Now Robbie had lots of friends visiting him but usually they were noisy and loud and raced around his bedroom taking no notice of the fish swimming in the fish tank.

However, Robbie's cousin was different. His name was Alex and he wasn't loud, he wasn't noisy and he didn't race around Robbie's bedroom. But he did take a big interest in Robbie's fish tank.

"I love all your fish, Robbie!" he declared as soon as he set eyes on them. "I've always wanted an aquarium of my own. You are so lucky to have so many beautiful fish!"

"You can have some if you want!" Robbie answered.

"Really?" asked Alex. "Are you sure you would want to give some away?"

"Yeah!" Robbie replied. "There's too many in there anyway. And dad told me that it would be a good idea to get rid of a couple because it's too crowded. Plus they're always hungry and I get tired of always having to feed them!"

"Wow!" said Alex. "I would love that! And I wouldn't mind feeding them at all!"

"We have a spare fish tank in the garage as well," said Robbie. "I'll ask my parents if you can have it. It may as well get used."

"Oh, this is my lucky day!" exclaimed Alex. "Thanks Robbie!"

The fish in the aquarium looked at Alex and they looked at Robbie. They all wondered who the lucky fish would be. And they all hoped that they would be the ones to go and live with Alex in a new uncrowded fish tank with plenty to eat.

"You can have any fish except the rainbow sharks," said Robbie. "They're my favorite ones, but you can choose any two of the others."

"I think I like that pretty goldfish," said Alex. "She's so beautiful!"

Gus looked on in horror. Was Alex going to take Gina away from him? He didn't know if he would survive in the tank without her. He felt sure that he would die from loneliness if Gina left.

"And I also like that red finned fish," said Alex. "He's so fast!"

Alex grabbed the net that lay on the table and quickly scooped up Gina as she tried to hide beside Gus amongst the weeds. He carefully plopped her into a bag full of water that Gus had handed to him.

Gina swam frantically around the bag, desperately looking out at Gus and hoping for a miracle.

Alex scooped the net through the water once more, trying to catch the speedy little red finned fish. But after a few attempts, he still hadn't caught him. "Here," said Robbie. "Let me have a go. I'll catch him for you!" However, the red fin proved to be way too quick for Robbie as well.

"It doesn't matter," said Alex, as he scooped the net into the water one last time. "I don't mind which fish I have. I love all of the fish and I'll be happy with any one of them." Then in the blink of an eye, before Alex was able to capture any of the other fish in the tank, Gus swam quickly into the net. And Alex lifted it carefully out of the water and gently popped Gus into the bag with Gina.

Smiling shyly, Gus swam beside her and fanned out his rainbow colored fins. He was overwhelmed with happiness and joy.

Finally he was going to have the life that he had dreamed of. He was going to live in a roomy tank, with plenty of food and be looked after by an owner who was kind and caring. But the best part of all was that his special friend Gina would be there with him.

Gus was the most grateful fish on the planet.

He knew right then that his dream really had come true!

Tommy the Little Turtle

Tommy was a little turtle. He lived with his mom and his dad and his granddad. They all loved Tommy very much. He was a very special turtle. He had a smooth shiny shell, four little legs and the biggest smile that you have ever seen; especially for a little turtle. His smile was so wide that everyone smiled when they saw him. He was such a happy little turtle, that everyone felt happy when they saw his huge smile. It instantly made everyone else want to smile as well.

There was just one problem. Tommy was very, very slow. Now, we all know that turtles never move very quickly but Tommy was even slower than the slowest turtle. In fact, he was probably the slowest turtle ever!

But his mom never got cross with him, even when he couldn't keep up. She just called out, "Hurry up Tommy! Hurry up, or you will get left behind!" And Tommy would try to hurry.

Sometimes Tommy went out for a walk with his granddad. Now his granddad was very slow, but even he would have to call out, "Hurry up, Tommy! Hurry up or you'll get left behind!" And Tommy would try to hurry. But because Tommy was such a happy little turtle his granddad never got cross with him, even when he couldn't keep up. He just sat down patiently and waited for Tommy to catch up to him.

Sometimes, Tommy's dad took him to the park to play on the playground. But Tommy walked so slowly, that it would take them a long time to get there. Once again, because Tommy was such a happy little turtle his dad never got cross with him, even when he couldn't keep up. Instead, he just called out, "Hurry up Tommy! Hurry up or you'll get left behind!"

Although Tommy tried very hard to be quicker, it was no use. He just couldn't do it. He was the slowest turtle ever.

One day, when Tommy was out with his family, they decided to go for a walk through the woods. They had never been to this particular part of the woods before but they'd heard that it had a lovely swimming hole.

And they thought that Tommy would really enjoy having a swim there.

Because they all knew how slow Tommy was, they

decided to leave very early. They had a long way to go and they wanted to get there by lunch time. They took a picnic basket and all of Tommy's favorite treats. Tommy was very excited. And Tommy's mom and dad were excited. Even Tommy's granddad was excited. It was going to be a lot of fun.

After walking for what seemed like a very long time, they finally arrived at the woods. Tommy was very, very excited. He could see beautiful flowers and beautiful butterflies and beautiful birds. In fact, there were so many beautiful things everywhere he looked, that it was very hard to concentrate on where he was going.

Suddenly he saw a beautiful blue butterfly and decided to follow it. The problem was that he wasn't watching where he was going as he was too busy following the beautiful blue butterfly. Then it abruptly disappeared from sight. "Where has that beautiful blue butterfly gone?" he thought to himself. But it was nowhere to be seen.

As Tommy looked around, he suddenly thought about his mom and his dad and his granddad. He looked behind him to see if he could see them. But they weren't there. He looked ahead of him to see if he could see them. But they weren't there. He looked to the left and to the right to see if he could see them. But they weren't there.

"Where is my family?" he thought to himself. He called to his mom. He called to his dad. He called to his granddad. But there was no answer. Tommy started to worry.

"Have you seen my family?" he asked a rainbow colored butterfly that landed on his nose. "No, I haven't," said the rainbow colored butterfly.

Have you seen my family?" he asked a beautiful red bird that landed on the ground at his feet. "No, I haven't," said the beautiful red bird.

"Have you seen my family?" he asked a little grey bunny that was hopping by. "No, I haven't," said the little grey bunny as it stopped beside him.

"I think I'm lost!" exclaimed Tommy to the butterfly and the bird and the bunny. "I need to find my family!" he cried.

"I will help you," said the rainbow colored butterfly.

"I will help you," said the beautiful red bird.

"I will help you," said the little grey bunny.

"Thank you!" said Tommy and he smiled his biggest smile that went from one side of his face to the other. When Tommy's new friends saw his beautiful big smile, they smiled too. "Yes, of course, we will help you!" they all cried.

So they headed down the forest path, looking for Tommy's family.

"Hurry up, Tommy," said the rainbow colored butterfly. "Or you'll get left behind!"

"Hurry up, Tommy," said the beautiful red bird, "Or you'll get left behind!"

"Hurry up, Tommy," said the little grey bunny, "Or you'll get left behind!"

"I'm trying to hurry," said Tommy with a huge smile on his face as he tried his very hardest not to be quite so slow. Because Tommy was such a happy little turtle, his friends were very patient with him and just took their time. "Don't worry, Tommy!" they all said. "We'll help you find your family!"

It was very lucky for Tommy because his friends knew the way to the water hole and they were able to take him in the right direction. It took a long time, because Tommy was very slow, but eventually they got there.

And there was Tommy's family sitting by the waterhole waiting for him to arrive.

"There you are, Tommy!" exclaimed his mother.

"There you are Tommy!" exclaimed his father.

"There you are Tommy!" exclaimed his granddad.

"We thought you'd never get here!" they all cried.

And Tommy smiled his widest smile. He was so happy to see his family again.

Tommy's family smiled at Tommy.

The rainbow colored butterfly smiled at Tommy.

The beautiful red bird smiled at Tommy.

And the little grey bunny smiled at Tommy.

Everyone was very happy.

Tommy and his family had a lovely swim in the beautiful water hole while Tommy's new friends sat and watched them. Then Tommy and his family decided it was time to go home.

That was one of the most exciting days I've ever had," said Tommy to his family. "Can we come back tomorrow?"

"Maybe not tomorrow," said Tommy's mom.

"Maybe one day next week," said Tommy's dad.

"Or maybe the week after that," said Tommy's granddad.

"Well please come back soon!" said Tommy's new friends.

"We will!" said Tommy, as he waved goodbye. "Thank you for helping me today!" he called. "We will be back soon, I promise."

And Tommy smiled his widest smile and he and his family headed home.

The Lonely Dinosaur

Once upon a time, there was a dinosaur named Danni. Danni wasn't any ordinary dinosaur. She had very big eyes, a very long neck and a very long tail that curved a bit at the end. But the most special thing about Danni was that she was always very, very kind and very, very friendly.

There was just one problem. Danny was lonely! Now you'd think that because she was so kind and so friendly, she would have lots of friends to play with, but this just wasn't the case. Even though Danni tried very, very hard to be kind and friendly, she still had no one to play with.

So one day, she decided to go on a long walk to see if she could find some friends who would play with her.

First of all, she spotted at tiger sitting on a log. Danni thought that the tiger looked friendly, so she asked, "Can I play with you?"

"No, you can't play with me!" said the tiger sitting on the log. "You're way too tall!"

So Danni moved on until she found a brown and white dog with four white legs. "Can I play with you?" she asked the large brown and white dog with four white legs.

"No, you can't play with me," said the large dog. "Your tail is too long and I am too busy riding my skateboard."

So Danni kept walking until she found a yellow lion with golden fur. "Can I play with you?" Danni asked the yellow lion with golden fur.

"No, you can't play with me!" said the yellow lion. "Your eyes are too big and I'm playing with my friend the zebra."

So Danni walked on further still until she found a fat, pink pig.

"Can I play with you?" she asked the fat, pink pig.

"No, you can't play with me," said the fat, pink pig. "Your neck is too long! And besides, I'm busy sleeping!"

Danni stopped and sat down. She sighed a huge sigh. She felt lonelier than ever. It seemed that everyone had a friend except her and she was very sad.

"Why won't anyone play with me?" she asked herself sadly. "I try to be friendly, I try to be nice and I try to be kind, but still no one will play with me."

"It must be because I look so different to all the other animals," she decided. "I am too tall. My neck and my tail are too long. I must look very strange, because no one wants to play with me and no one wants to be my friend."

Danni the dinosaur started to cry. She didn't know what to do.

After a while, she got up and decided to keep walking. She knew that she couldn't give up! Surely she would be able to find a friend somewhere who would want to play with her.

But before long the sun started to set and the sky began to grow dark.

Danni became scared. She wasn't used to being out at night on her own. She knew that she really should go back home as her parents would be very worried about her. But she was determined not to go back until she had found a friend.

"Hoot, hoot!" called an owl, as it sat on a tree branch watching Danni walk past. "Who are you and where have you come from?" asked the owl.

"I'm trying to find a friend so I'll have someone to

play with," Danni explained.

"Why don't you have any friends?" the owl asked Danni.

"Because I am too tall, my neck and tail are too long and my eyes are too big," Danni replied. "No one wants to be my friend because I look so strange!" she continued sadly. "And no one wants to play with me."

"I don't think your eyes are too big!" said the owl.

"You don't?" asked Danni, in a surprised voice.

"Not at all," replied the owl. "Look at my eyes; they are much bigger than yours."

All of a sudden, along strolled a giraffe. "Who are you and where have you come from?" asked the giraffe curiously.

"I'm trying to find a friend so I'll have someone to play with," Danni explained.

"Why don't you have any friends?" the giraffe asked Danni.

"Because I am too tall, my neck and tail are too long and my eyes are too big," Danni replied. "No one wants to be my friend because I look so strange!" she said with a sigh. "And no one wants to play with me."

"I don't think you're too tall or your neck is too

long!" said the giraffe.

"You don't?" asked Danni, in a surprised voice.

"Not at all," replied the giraffe. "Look how tall I am; I am much taller than you. And my neck is much longer as well!"

All of a sudden, across the grassland hopped a kangaroo. "Who are you and where have you come from?" asked the kangaroo curiously.

"I'm trying to find a friend so I'll have someone to play with," Danni explained.

"Why don't you have any friends?" the kangaroo asked Danni.

"Because I am too tall, my neck and tail are too long and my eyes are too big," Danni replied. "No one wants to be my friend because I look so strange!" she explained unhappily. "And no one wants to play with me."

"I don't think your tail is too long!" said the kangaroo.

"You don't?" asked Danni, in a surprised voice.

"Not at all," replied the kangaroo. "Look how long my tail is. It is much longer than yours!"

Then just as Danni was about to sit down and think about what the animals had said to her, along stomped a huge, grey elephant.

"Who are you and where have you come from?" asked the elephant curiously.

"I'm trying to find a friend so I'll have someone to play with," Danni explained.

"Why don't you have any friends?" the elephant asked Danni.

"Because I am too tall, my neck and tail are too long and my eyes are too big," Danni replied. "No one wants to be my friend because I look so strange!" she explained unhappily. "And no one wants to play with me."

"I don't think you are too tall, or that your neck and tail are too long or that your eyes are too big!" said the elephant. "In fact, I don't think that you look strange at all!"

"You don't?" asked Danni, in a hopeful voice.

"Not at all," replied the elephant. "Look how big my eyes are! And look how big my ears are! And look how big my trunk is!" he declared. "And I have lots of friends!"

"You do?" asked Danny. "You are so lucky! I wish I had lots of friends."

"I'll be your friend!" said the elephant.

"I'll be your friend!" said the kangaroo.

"I'll be your friend!" said the giraffe.

"I'll be your friend!" said the owl.

"Really?" asked Danni. "Will you really be my friends?"

"Yes," they all cried. "You seem very friendly and you seem very kind. We would love to be your friends."

Danny was shocked. They actually wanted to be her friends. She didn't know what to say.

She sat down next to her new friends with a huge smile and a happy feeling inside. She felt happier than she had ever felt before. Finally she had found some animals who didn't think she looked strange. They didn't care that she was too tall or that her neck and tail were too long or that her eyes were too big. In fact, they didn't care what she looked like at all. She had searched and searched and finally she had found some friends who liked her just the way she was. All they seemed to care about was that she was very friendly and very kind.

"So that's the way to make friends," Danny thought to herself. "As long as you are friendly and kind, I think you can have lots of friends. You just have to look for the right ones. The ones who like you just the way you are!"

And from that day onwards, Danni was never lonely again.

Captain Peg Leg

and

The Shy Penguin Pirate

Captain Peg Leg was a pirate. He had a scruffy orange beard, a hook for a hand, a shiny sharp silver cutlass and a wooden peg leg.

Now some pirates are mean and nasty but Captain Peg Leg was meaner and nastier than most. In fact, he was so mean and nasty that all the other pirates tried to stay away from him.

But Captain Peg Leg hadn't always been that mean. You see one time many years ago he had been sailing the seven seas looking for buried treasure, he had come across a very large, very ferocious alligator. And that alligator was guarding the spot where the treasure lay hidden.

Captain Peg Leg knew that the treasure was buried there because it said so on his treasure map. And he was determined to claim that treasure as his own. He had been searching for it for years and years and had finally discovered the hiding place. It was buried in the middle of a very small island that was right in the middle of a very muddy swamp.

But every day and every night, the very large, very ferocious alligator circled the swamp, his eyes appearing just above the surface of the muddy water, making sure that the treasure stayed safe and sound.

When Captain Peg Leg realized that the very large, very ferocious alligator was going to be a problem, he devised a plan.

He decided to wait until it got dark then he would hop into his little row boat, row quietly to the little island in the middle of the swamp and dig for the buried treasure.

Everything was going smoothly and Captain Peg Leg felt sure that the treasure would soon be his. But he underestimated the very large, very ferocious alligator that had been secretly watching him from the depths of the muddy water.

And with one whack of his mighty tail, the crocodile whipped the little row boat into the air and Captain Peg Leg ended up in the swamp.

He had to swim very quickly back to his pirate ship

but this was extremely difficult as he had a hook for a hand and a peg leg. He had lost his hand and his leg in an accident many years before and he certainly didn't want to lose his remaining hand or leg; or even worse still, be gobbled up by the alligator.

But maybe the alligator wasn't hungry or maybe the water was just too muddy. Or maybe he just wanted to scare Captain Peg Leg and keep him away from the island in the middle of the swamp and the buried treasure. Because Captain Peg Leg managed to make it safely back to his pirate ship.

Now, he should have been very grateful for this, but for Captain Peg Leg, it was the last straw.

He was tired of having a hook for a hand. He was tired of having a peg leg. And he was tired of not being able to find the buried treasure.

This made him very upset. In fact it made him so upset that he became meaner than ever. And he started to bully all the other pirates.

"Get to work!" he said gruffly to the pirates on the pirate ship.

"I am the Captain of this ship and you must do what I say!" he roared each day.

Now some of the other pirates were also mean and nasty and some were not. But regardless, they all raced to do whatever Captain Peg Leg told them to do, because he was such a bully.

Even his own parrot became scared of him!

"Scrub the decks!" Captain Peg Leg roared to all the

pirates.

"Tie the ropes!" he yelled. "And repair the wooden plank or you'll end up in the muddy swamp with the alligator!"

He gave them orders every day and every day he became meaner and nastier and more of a bully.

But one day, Captain Peg Leg decided to sail back across the seven seas because he had given up on getting past the very large, very ferocious alligator that guarded the buried treasure.

He had decided that it was time to go ashore and find some new pirates for his pirate ship. He was tired of the pirates on his ship and he wanted some new pirates to boss around.

Captain Peg Leg found that there were many pirates to choose from and they were all looking for a new ship and a new captain.

Of course, they didn't realize that Captain Peg Leg was such a bully and they were all very keen to be chosen.

There were even other pirates with a hook for a hand or a peg leg. It seems that this is the way it goes with many pirates.

But one pirate that was chosen, happened to be a penguin, named Paul. He was quite a shy pirate and Captain Peg Leg thought that he would be very easy to bully.

"Scrub the decks!" Captain Peg Leg roared as soon as the ship set sail.

"Tie the ropes!" he yelled to Paul, the penguin pirate and all the other pirates on board. "Repair the wooden plank or you'll end up being thrown into the sea!"

He gave them orders every day and every day he became meaner and nastier and more of a bully.

The pirates all grew very sad and very upset. Even the mean pirates started to become concerned. They didn't like being bullied by Captain Peg Leg but no one knew what to do.

Then one day, something happened and this surprised all the pirates on board the ship. In fact, it surprised Captain Peg Leg the most!

Paul, the penguin pirate decided to stand up to Captain Peg Leg. He had had enough of his bullying and he couldn't take it anymore. He knew that someone had to do something or they would all continue to suffer. And even though some of the pirates on board the ship were quite mean themselves, no one was brave enough to stand up to Captain Peg Leg.

Paul, the penguin pirate took a deep breath and puffed out his chest. He tried his hardest to look confident and brave and walked straight up to Captain Peg Leg.

"Captain Peg Leg," he said, "The other pirates and I are tired of the way you speak to us and we are tired of your bullying. We do not like it and we want you to stop!" He used his most confident sounding voice, even though he was really shaking inside with fear, but he made sure that Captain Peg Leg did not see this.

"Ha!" said the Captain. "Who do you think you are, talking to me like that?" he demanded.

Captain Peg Leg spluttered with surprise. No one had ever spoken to him like that before. No one had ever stood up to him before. And he wasn't sure what to do.

This shy little penguin appeared to be very confident and Captain Peg Leg could see that he wasn't going to be pushed around anymore.

He looked at Paul thoughtfully and said, "You are very brave to talk to me like that and I respect you for being strong and being able to stand up for yourself. I will not bully you anymore!

All the other pirates on board the ship started to cheer. "Hooray for Paul!" they cried. "Hooray for Paul, the penguin pirate!"

And from that day onwards, a very strange thing happened. Captain Peg Leg stopped being mean, he stopped being nasty and he stopped bullying the pirates. In fact, he stopped his bullying altogether.

And all it had taken was for a shy little penguin pirate to become confident and brave. By standing up to that bully, Paul had solved the problem. And he and the other pirates were never bullied again!

The Reindeer Race

Rex was a little reindeer who lived at the North Pole with his family. Ever since he was born, Rex had always been small. He was the tiniest baby, anyone had ever seen. But his mom always said to him, "You may be tiny, but you are very, very special. You're the most special reindeer of all!"

At first, Rex didn't mind being so small. He knew that his parents loved him. He knew that his brothers and sisters all loved him and he knew that he was very lucky to have such a wonderful family.

There were also lots of other young reindeer in the woods for Rex to play with. And every day as soon as they woke up and had breakfast, they would head out to play. Their favorite game of all was to race each other through the snow all the way to Santa's house and then back to the woods where they lived. Every day they would play this game and every day Rex was sure that he was getting faster.

The problem for Rex was that because he was so small, he always had trouble keeping up with them. And although he tried very, very hard, he never seemed to be able to win the races. "It's because you're so small!" his friends teased. "You'll never be able to win, Rex! You're just too little!"

Rex didn't really care that he never won, as racing with his friends was so much fun. The thing that worried him the most was that Santa would soon be looking out for the fastest reindeer to pull his sleigh. And Rex knew that if he wasn't able to run fast, then Santa would not choose him.

Every day, the reindeer raced and every day Rex tried harder and harder. He was so determined to become faster, that he decided he would not give up.

"Poor little Rex," his mom whispered to the other moms who were watching the races. "He desperately wants to become faster but it's very hard for him as he is so much smaller than all the other reindeer! I wish I could help him," she sighed.

The other moms looked on with pity. You see everyone liked Rex because he was such a friendly, happy little reindeer and they all thought that he deserved a spot on Santa's team. However, they could see it was going to be very difficult for him.

But Rex had decided he would not give up. So each day, he practiced running. He woke up very early and went out into the woods before anyone else had woken. And he practiced and he practiced. He ran to Santa's house and back to the woods several times before breakfast and then again several times before dinner. He had decided that if he practiced and didn't give up, then surely he would improve.

Each day, Rex did this and each day, the other reindeer laughed at him. "Rex!" they called. "Why do you bother? Why don't you just give up?" They all laughed and snickered as they ran quickly past him.

But Rex ignored them. He was determined to do his best and just keep on trying.

Then one day, Santa came out into the woods. It was the day that the reindeer had all been waiting for. "I need to find a new reindeer to pull the sleigh this year," Santa said.

"One of my reindeer is getting too old and weak so I need a new reindeer to replace him."

"All the young reindeer listened carefully to Santa. Ever since they were born, they had admired the very special reindeer that pulled Santa's sleigh at Christmas time. And every Christmas eve, they would sit with their families and watch as the sleigh was filled with presents for all the good girls and boys. It was very exciting to watch the reindeer take off into the night sky as Santa called out, "Ho! Ho! Ho! Merry Christmas!"

The reindeer who pulled the sleigh were Santa's very special helpers and they had such an important job to do. Without them, Santa would never be able to deliver all the presents and Christmas would not happen.

"Rudolph will be helping me to choose a new reindeer for my team!" Santa continued. "We have decided to hold a special race so we can watch to see who the fastest reindeer is. But we're looking for other qualities as well," Santa explained further.

"You see, to be on my team is an honor and we need one new reindeer that is reliable and hard working as well as fast. We will be watching you all so that we can make the right choice!"

Rudolph explained the details of the race to all the young reindeer. It was going to be a very long race and there were lots of directions that the reindeer needed to listen to.

"This won't be a problem for me!" scoffed Reggie, the fastest reindeer of them all, as he strutted past Rex. "And surely Rex, you're not going to bother trying? What hope do you have?"

Rex decided to ignore Reggie's rude comment and concentrated on listening to Rudolph's instructions because he knew that they were very important.

The race was going to be held the very next day and the woods were abuzz with excitement. Everyone was talking about the competition and several reindeer had already decided that they were going to win.

Rex didn't say anything. He just walked quietly home, thinking about the race and planning on getting up bright and early in the morning so that he would be ready.

The very next day, all the young reindeer waited impatiently at the starting line. The race track went deep into the woods and they all knew that they had a big race ahead.

Rudolph called out, "Ready, Set, Go!" and the reindeer all took off, in a flash. There was a cloud of white snow that had been kicked up by their hooves but when it finally cleared, all the spectators could see were the tails of the reindeer as they raced deep into the woods out of sight.

But then one of the onlookers yelled, "Look, it's Rex! He's still on the open track. He's *way* behind all the others!"

As Rex raced along, all he could see in front of him was a blur of white snow as the other reindeer ran quickly ahead. But Rex just put his head down and kept on running.

Along the track he ran, deep into the woods, following behind all the other reindeer, with Reggie in the lead. On and on, the reindeer all ran, over frozen rivers and through thick woodlands, on and on along the track.

Then all of a sudden Reggie came to a fork in the track. He stopped and looked behind him. He had managed to get ahead of the others and felt very confident that he was going to win. But he realized that he didn't know which path to take. He tried to remember what Rudolph had told them all the day before. He knew that he hadn't been listening very well and now he wasn't sure which track was the right one.

He could hear the hooves of the other reindeer pounding on the ground behind him and knew that he had to act quickly if he wanted to stay in the lead. So without another thought, he headed down the track that veered to the left.

Feeling confident that he had made the right choice, he raced on ahead, snow flying up all around him as he ran. The other reindeer weren't far behind and could see the cloud of white snow that had been stirred up amongst the trees on the track ahead of them. So without any hesitation, they veered to the left following along the path that Reggie had taken. After all, he was the fastest reindeer of them all and if he had chosen that track, then it must be the right one.

Along the track the reindeer all ran, over more frozen rivers and through more thick woodland. On and on and on they went.

Meanwhile Rex, who had continued on at his usual steady pace, finally came to the fork in the track. He slowed down to a stop and took time to think about the two choices ahead of him. But then he remembered Rudolph's instructions the day before. "When you come to the fork in the track, be sure to take the path on the right. That will lead you straight to the finish line," he had explained to all of the reindeer.

Because Rex had been listening so carefully, he remembered Rudolph's words and without any hesitation whatsoever, raced along in the direction that he had been told.

Steadily on, Rex ran, as fast as his little legs would carry him. On and on and on he ran until eventually, up ahead he could see the Finish Line. But to his surprise, he could not see any of the other reindeer and wondered if he were the last one to get there.

But still he pushed on, the Finish Line in sight along with Santa and Rudolph and all the spectators cheering him on. "Run, Rex! Run!" the voices all cried.

"Were they actually calling his name?" he wondered to himself as he raced tirelessly, his little legs running as fast as they could go.

When he raced across the line with none of the other young reindeer in sight, he couldn't believe it as Santa and Rudolph approached him, huge smiles on their faces.

Then suddenly, out of nowhere, a thundering sound could be heard. Everyone turned abruptly to look down the track and saw a cloud of white snow and a herd of reindeer racing for the finish line. As they approached at lightning speed with Reggie in the lead, the spectators quickly cleared out of their path.

Strutting proudly over to Santa and Rudolph, completely confident that he had won, Reggie exclaimed proudly to everyone there, "I knew that I would win!"

But Santa and Rudolph walked straight past him, towards the crowd of onlookers where Rex was still standing.

"Congratulations, Rex!" exclaimed Santa. "You have won the race!"

"But I'm the fastest reindeer and I got here first!" stammered Reggie, extremely surprised at the sight of Rex standing in the crowd.

"No, you didn't!" explained Santa. "And not only is Rex the winner of the race, but he's also the best listener and the hardest worker. He's the one little reindeer who tries his hardest all the time and never gives up! That's the sort of reindeer I want for my team!"

And as Reggie stood stock still, overcome with shock, Rex stood tall and proud. His mom had always said that he was a very special reindeer and now he had proved it. He had earned his place on Santa's team.

"Slow and steady wins the race," thought Rex, as he stood there with a huge beaming smile lighting up his happy face.

And right then, he was the proudest little reindeer that ever lived!

Are You My Mommy?

One day a fluffy, little, yellow chick pecked her way out of a hard egg shell and hopped out into the world for the very first time.

As she looked curiously around at her unfamiliar surroundings, the first animal that she spotted was a very big, very fat, very round and very, very pink pig.

"Oink, oink!" said the very big, very fat, very round, very, very pink pig.

"Are you my mommy?" asked the fluffy, little, yellow chick.

"Oink, oink!" repeated the very big, very fat, very round, very, very pink pig. "No, I am not your mommy. I am a pig!"

"I must find my mommy!" said the little chick. "Will you please help me find her?"

"Yes, I will help you!" said the pig. And off they went.

The very big, very fat, very round, very, very pink pig walked with the fluffy, little, yellow chick down the dusty road until eventually they came to a field. In the field stood a large, brown horse with a curly, brown tail.

"Neigh!" said the large brown horse with a curly brown tail.

"Are you my mommy?" asked the fluffy, little, yellow chick.

"Neigh!" repeated the large, brown horse with a curly brown tail. "No, I am not your mommy. I am a horse!"

"I must find my mommy!" said the little chick. "Will you please help me find her?"

"Yes, I will help you!" said the horse. And off they went.

So, the large, brown horse with a curly, brown tail and the very big, very fat, very round, very, very pink pig walked with the fluffy, little, yellow chick down the dusty road until eventually they came to a pond.

By the pond, stood a friendly goose with white feathers and large, webbed feet.

"Honk! Honk!" said the friendly goose with white feathers and large, webbed feet.

"Are you my mommy?" asked the fluffy, little, yellow chick.

"Honk! Honk!" repeated the friendly goose with white feathers and large, webbed feet. "No, I am not your mommy. I am a goose!"

"I must find my mommy!" said the little chick. "Will you please help me find her?"

"Yes, I will help you!" said the goose. And off they went.

So, the friendly goose with white feathers and large, webbed feet and the large, brown horse with a curly brown tail and the very big, very fat, very round, very, very pink pig all walked with the fluffy, little, yellow chick down the dusty road until eventually they came to a tall tree.

Under the tall tree, stood a donkey with long, pointy ears and a loud voice.

"Eee Aww! Eee Aww!" said the donkey with long, pointy ears and a loud voice.

"Are you my mommy?" asked the fluffy, little, yellow chick.

"Eee Aww!" repeated the donkey with long, pointy ears and a loud voice. "No, I am not your mommy. I am a donkey!"

"I must find my mommy!" said the little chick. "Will you please help me find her?"

"Yes, I will help you!" said the donkey. And off they went.

So, the donkey with long, pointy ears and a loud voice and the friendly goose with white feathers and large, webbed feet and the large, brown horse with a curly brown tail and the very big, very fat, very round, very, very pink pig all walked with the fluffy, little, yellow chick down the dusty road until eventually they came to a barn.

"This barn looks familiar!" said the very big, very fat, very round, very, very pink pig.

"I think this is my barn!" he continued with surprise. "I wonder how we got back here!"

All the animals followed the very big, very fat, very round, very, very pink pig into the barn where they found a hen resting with her chicks.

"Are you my mommy?" asked the fluffy, little, yellow chick.

"Yes, of course I am your mommy!" exclaimed the hen. "Where have you been? I have been looking for you everywhere!"

"Mommy!" cried the fluffy, little, yellow chick as he raced towards her. "I am so glad to have found you! I will never leave you again!"

And from that day onwards, the fluffy, little, yellow chick stayed right by her mother's side.

That was of course, until she grew up to be a big chicken herself. But that's a whole different adventure!

The Naughty Little Goat

High on a hill, up a steep, rocky path was a little village. And in that village lived a family of goats. But this wasn't any ordinary family. In fact, this family was quite extraordinary. And that was because this particular family was full of goats that were all shapes and sizes.

There were big goats and little goats and fat goats and skinny goats and goats with beards and goats with horns. Some of them had long, pointy horns and some of them had long, curved horns and some of them had no horns whatsoever. But they all lived happily together in the little village, up the steep, rocky path, high on the hill.

Each day, the family of goats would get up early and go looking for some sweet grass to eat. There was a special spot on one side of the mountain where a river flowed and the grass grew long and green.

It was the goats' favorite place to eat. But it was a long, long walk from the village and there were many steep and rocky paths to climb.

Luckily for the goats, they were all very good at climbing. Their hooves were strong and they were able to balance easily on the narrow tracks and rocky paths. These were the paths that covered the side of the mountain leading to the sweet, sweet grass that grew long and green by the side of the river.

There was just one small problem! Gerry, the smallest goat of all, was a very cheeky little goat and also very naughty. He was so naughty in fact that he would often stray away from the rest of his family and race along another steep path that criss-crossed the side of the mountain. Then someone would have to go looking for him in case he got lost.

"Please stay with us today, Gerry!" said his brothers each day. "We are walking on the steep rocky path up high on the hill so we can get to our favorite place to eat and we don't want you to get lost."

"OK," replied Gerry in his cheeky little voice. "I'll stay with you today!"

And then sure enough, when no one was looking, Gerry would run off in the other direction.

Eventually, his brothers got so frustrated with him that they decided to keep on walking. When Gerry realized that they weren't going to chase after him, he knew he would have to get their attention in another way.

"Help me! Help me!" he cried out loudly and then ran to hide behind a bush waiting for his brothers to come and find him.

Sure enough, his brothers came running. They were very worried that Gerry had hurt himself. "Gerry, Gerry!" they called. "Where are you?"

And Gerry jumped out from behind the bush. He grinned his cheeky grin and yelled, "Here I am!"

"Oh Gerry!" his brothers roused. "You're so cheeky! You're so naughty! We thought you had been hurt! Please don't do that again!"

And off they went, up the steep, rocky path in search of the sweet, sweet grass that grew by the river on the steepest part of the hill.

The very next day, the family of goats set off once more, bright and early, in search of their favorite grass to eat. And once more, Gerry raced off in the other direction.

This time, his brothers decided that he needed to learn a lesson so they just kept on walking.

Once again, Gerry realized they weren't coming after him. So he hid behind a bush and called out loudly, "Help me! Help me! I've hurt myself. Please come and help me!"

And once again, Gerry's brothers were so concerned that they all raced back to look for him, very worried that he had been injured.

Gerry jumped out from behind the bush, grinned his cheeky grin and yelled, "Here I am!"

But this time, his brothers were very upset with him! They were tired of Gerry being cheeky. They were tired of Gerry being naughty. And they were tired of

Gerry making up stories.

"If you do that again Gerry, we won't believe you and we will not come back for you!" they declared.

But Gerry, just trotted happily along on the track behind them, pleased that he had managed to trick them once more.

After feasting on the sweet, green grass that grew long and tall by the side of the river, the goats headed back home.

"Please stay with us this time, Gerry," they said to him. "If you make up stories again, we will not believe you!"

And back down the hill they all trotted.

Just as the sun was about to set and they had almost arrived back at the village, Gerry decided that he would try his trick one last time. He raced off in the other direction and hid behind a bush.

"Help me! Help me!" he cried loudly. "I've been injured. I need your help!"

His brothers heard him call. They heard him call out loudly. They heard him call out clearly. But they had decided they'd had enough of Gerry's stories and this time, he really did need to learn a lesson once and for all.

So they kept on walking.

Gerry waited and waited behind the bush, but his brothers did not come, so he called out again. "Help me! Help me!" he called out loudly and he called out clearly. "I've been injured. I need your help!"

But to Gerry's surprise, his brothers still did not come.

Just as he was about to give up and head down towards the village on his own, he heard a strange voice. "Who are you, my little friend?"

When Gerry turned around to see who was speaking to him, he realized that he was in trouble. The voice had come from a fierce looking lion with a yellow mane. And the lion was staring fiercely at Gerry.

Gerry knew that his brothers weren't coming to help him. He knew that he had been too cheeky. He knew that he had been too naughty and he knew that he had told too many stories. They did not believe him and they wanted to teach him a lesson.

Gerry stood shaking in fear. He did not know what to do!

"Please don't eat me!" he whimpered to the fierce looking lion.

But to Gerry's huge relief, the lion replied, "You are a very lucky little goat! I have just had my dinner and I'm not hungry. Otherwise I would eat you up right now in one big gulp!"

The lion moved closer and said to Gerry in a fierce voice, "You should not be walking on the mountain paths on your own! You are a very naughty and very silly little goat. You should go home right now before another lion comes along and eats you up!"

And without a moment's hesitation, Gerry raced off down the rocky path towards the village. As soon as he saw his family, he dropped down beside them with relief. "I was nearly eaten by a very fierce lion!" he cried. "And you didn't come to help me!"

"Gerry!" his brothers demanded. "We don't believe you. You tell too many stories and are way too cheeky. If you want us to believe you, you must start telling the truth!"

Gerry was still shaking with fear. He went to bed and thought long and hard about being so cheeky, about being so naughty and about making up stories. He decided that he had learned his lesson. He decided that he must be a good little goat and always tell the truth.

And from that day on, he never made up another story again.

Pete the Dragon Slayer

There was once a boy named Pete. And Pete had a very active imagination. His mind was full of adventures and action and all day long he pretended that he was someone else.

One day he pretended that he was a knight; a knight in shining armor galloping by on his horse, ready to save the kingdom from evil.

He thrust his sword from its sheath and galloped through the house, slaying all the dragons in his path. Until eventually the kingdom was safe and he could return to his castle.

"Be careful, Pete!" called his mom as he raced past the kitchen waving a cricket bat in the air. "Please stop swinging that bat. You might break something!"

"But I have to save the kingdom!" he yelled. "There are evil dragons everywhere!"

And on he raced, past the kitchen, down the hallway and into his bedroom, slamming the door behind him.

The next day, Pete pretended that he was an astronaut; an astronaut zooming through space in his speedy rocket racing to discover a new planet.

As he undid his seatbelt, he floated around in the cabin of his rocket and stared in wonder out the window at the shooting stars he could see falling through space.

"Look out!" he called to his mom. "You need to duck your head or the shooting stars will hit you!" he declared.

"Pete there are no shooting stars in our house!" replied his mom. "It's just your imagination!" But Pete ignored her and floated dreamily past, his hands clasped firmly above his head as his pretend rocket zoomed through the living room.

Then a week later, Pete pretended he was the captain of a pirate ship; a pirate who sailed across the seven seas, looking for an island with buried treasure. An eye patch covered one eye and he limped along on his wooden leg. He had lost his leg in a fight with a crocodile on his last visit to Treasure Island and he had replaced it with a wooden one instead.

"Aye, aye!" he shouted to his mom. "There's buried treasure ahead but we must be careful. We have to watch out for the crocodiles in the swamp!" And he limped along, heading towards the swimming pool in the back garden. "The treasure is buried right by that palm tree!" he declared, as he raced for the tool shed to find the shovel so he could begin digging.

"Pete!" his mom shouted back to him, a worried frown appearing on her face. "You're day dreaming again. Please put that shovel back in the shed. I'm worried you might hurt yourself!"

It was the same thing every day. Every day, Pete

woke up and pretended that he was someone else, someone adventurous and full of action and exciting. Just like one of the characters in his favorite book of fairy tales that his mom read to him each night.

At first his mom thought that it was just harmless fun. Pete had a vivid imagination and he was just play acting. But then she started to worry. She worried that Pete would forget that he was really a little boy called Pete. Not a knight in shining armor, racing through the forest, slaying evil dragons so he could save the kingdom. Not an astronaut zooming through space hoping to discover a new planet. And certainly not a pirate with a wooden leg and a patch over his eye, looking out for buried treasure.

So Pete's mom decided that she would put the book of adventure stories away for a while and find another book to read to Pete at night time before he went to sleep. She was hoping that would do the trick. She hoped Pete would remember that he was really Pete, a little boy who lived in a lovely little house with his mom and his dad and his baby brother.

At first, Pete missed the book of adventure stories that were so full of action. But his mom had found a wonderful book of fairy tales that he realized he enjoyed just as much. You see apart from play-acting,

Pete's favorite time of the day was when his mom sat next to him in bed each night and read him a special story.

And Pete could still use his vivid imagination, although he decided that maybe he wouldn't be quite so adventurous any more.

He knew that he was Pete; Pete who lived in a lovely little house with his mom and his dad and his baby brother.

And maybe next time, he would only slay one dragon instead of ten. And after that, he would avoid the shooting stars when he went into space.

Then he would stay away from the crocodile swamp and the buried treasure.

And even though he would still pretend to be a knight in shining armor and an astronaut zooming through space and a pirate looking for treasure, deep down he knew that it was just pretend and that he was really Pete.

Happily, he closed his eyes and dreamed of the characters in the fairy tale book that his mom had just read to him.

And he wondered who he would pretend to be tomorrow.

Sally's Surprise

Sally was a very happy, little girl. She lived with her mom and dad in a big house in a lovely street.

Their house was surrounded by beautiful trees, fabulous parks and a wonderful playground.

Each day when Sally woke up, she and her mom would prepare breakfast together.

They got up early and cooked pancakes or waffles or toast or eggs.

Each day it was something different but each day, Sally and her mom and dad sat down and enjoyed a delicious breakfast.

Then after they had all eaten and her dad had gone off to work, Sally helped her mom to clean up the dishes and they headed off to the wonderful playground that was situated just at the end of the street.

Sally loved the swings the best and her mom would push the swing so that Sally sailed high in the sky.

It was her favorite thing to do! She also loved to skip really fast.

When the weather was wet and they were unable to visit the park, Sally and her mom stayed at home and played there instead.

Sometimes they would do puzzles together, sometimes they would do painting and drawing together, sometimes they would play board games together and sometimes Sally's mom would just sit and read to her. Sally loved playing with her mom each day and was very happy.

Then one day, Sally's mom said that she had a big surprise for her.

"What can it be?" Sally wondered. "Is it a new doll?" she asked.

"No, that's not it!" her mom replied, smiling widely.

"Is it a new dress?" Sally asked curiously.

"No, that's not it!" her mom replied, smiling even more widely.

"Is it a new toy or a new game?" Sally asked, more curious than ever.

"No, that's not it!" her mom replied once more. "Do you want me to tell you what it is?"

"Yes please!" Sally cried. "Please tell me the surprise!"

"You are going to have a new baby brother or sister!" exclaimed Sally's mom joyfully.

"A new baby brother or sister!" Sally repeated. "But when?" she asked hopefully. "Will the baby arrive today?"

"No, for a while," smiled Sally's mom, "But we have lots to do to get ready," she explained.

Sally was more than willing to help. She loved helping her mom around the house. They always did things together and it was always fun.

"Will I be able to play with my new baby brother or

sister?" she asked her mom.

"No, not straight away," her mom explained further. "But there will be lots of jobs for you to do and it won't be long then you will be able to play together."

Sally was very excited. She loved doing jobs with her mom and she loved the thought of having a new baby brother or sister to play with. She really preferred to have a sister, but decided that she didn't mind if she had a brother. She could still play with him regardless.

The months passed by and Sally and her mom continued to cook breakfast each morning and visit the playground each day so that Sally could have a turn on the swings. And when the weather was wet, they stayed at home and played games together instead.

Sally loved cuddling up to her mom. She now had a very big belly and sometimes when Sally put her ear up close, she could even hear the baby's heartbeat. She was very, very excited. Soon she would have a new baby brother or sister to play with.

One day when Sally woke up, she raced into her parents' room, the same way that she did every morning, but they weren't there.

"Where can they be?" she wondered to herself as she made her way downstairs to find them.

But instead of finding her parents in the kitchen, she

found Grandma instead.

"Hello Sally!" Grandma exclaimed cheerfully when she saw her. "Your mom and dad are at the hospital. Your new baby brother or sister will soon be born. And we will go to visit later today. In the meantime, sit down and I'll cook you some breakfast."

Sally felt very excited. The day she had been waiting for had finally arrived. But she still didn't know if she would have a baby brother or a baby sister. And Grandma didn't know either. She couldn't wait to get to the hospital to see her surprise.

The baby was fast asleep when Sally and her grandma arrived. Sally rushed into the hospital room noisily, full of excitement and joy. She was expecting to hold the baby straight away. Over the last few months, she had been practicing with her dolls at home and knew exactly what to do.

"Ssshhh, Sally!" whispered her mom as Sally raced over to the cot where the baby lay sleeping. "We don't want you to wake him!"

"Him?" Sally asked. "So he's a boy!" Sally was a little disappointed. She had really been hoping for a baby sister. "Can I hold him?" she asked loudly.

"Sssshhh, Sally!" whispered her dad who was sitting nearby. "We don't want you to wake him!"

"You'll be able to hold him tomorrow, Sally," explained her mom gently and she pulled Sally towards her and gave her a big hug. This made Sally feel better and when she went to bed later that night, she dreamt about her new little brother and all the fun they would soon be having together.

However, when Sally's mom and the baby finally came home, Sally found that having a new baby brother wasn't the exciting and fun experience that she had been expecting.

To begin with, he cried a lot. When Sally tried to help by sitting down and holding him carefully, just the way that she had been practicing, he fussed and kicked and cried even louder.

Her mom asked if she would like to help change his diaper. But that was way too smelly and no fun at all.

And the worst part was that her mom didn't seem to have time for her anymore. When the baby was sleeping, her mom was either very busy cleaning up all the mess or having a sleep herself.

Sally felt sad. She loved her baby brother and thought that he was very special but she wanted someone to play with.

Then one night, a few days later, Sally woke up to hear the baby crying. She hopped out of bed and raced into his room. Her mom and dad were still sleeping. They hadn't heard his cries.

She sat down by his cot and held his hand. She whispered quietly in his ear and decided to sing him a little song. To Sally's surprise, he suddenly stopped crying. He looked at her with his big wide eyes and smiled. Sally smiled back. She felt very special inside. Finally she had been able to help. Her baby brother had stopped crying and for the very first time he was smiling back at her.

The next day, she told her mom what had happened and then asked if she could try holding him again. He lay quietly in her lap as she held him very carefully. Sally loved his big brown eyes and his beautiful smile. Then she cuddled up next to her mom and her little brother when he was feeding. Sally patted his head gently and watched in wonder. She felt very lucky to be the big sister of such a beautiful baby brother.

She even started to help her mom change his diapers. After a while she got used to the smell and didn't mind it so much after all. She had realized that having a baby brother really was very special and there was a lot that she could do to help look after him.

Her favorite time of the day was feeding time. That was when she would cuddle up to her mom while she fed the baby and read Sally a story. This was their special time together every day.

And on the weekends when her dad was at home, he spent lots of time playing with her. They even started walking the baby in the stroller down to the park at the end of the street, where Sally was able to play on the swings, just like she had always done.

As Sally sat on the swing one afternoon, a big smile on her face, she knew that it wouldn't be long and she would actually be able to play with her little brother. Maybe she'd be able to push him on the swing one day. Now that would be fun. She sailed high in the sky and smiled her widest smile.

She was a big sister now and had many special jobs to do. She felt proud and happy. Having a new baby brother was a very special surprise but being a big sister was the most special surprise of all.

The Very Friendly Dog
and the
Very Brave Cat

Hugo was a very, very friendly dog. He wagged his tail and flopped his ears and barked a very friendly bark. He was the friendliest dog that ever lived and also the most gentle.

Whenever he went for a walk, he ran up to people on the street, wagging his tail, flopping his ears and barking his friendliest bark. "Hello!" Hugo said, to anybody who would listen. "My name is Hugo. Will you pat me?"

You see, Hugo loved to be patted. He also loved to be talked to and he loved to be with people. He was the friendliest dog you could ever imagine. And as well as that, he was also the most playful!

One of the games that Hugo loved was to fetch a ball or a stick that had been thrown for him. "Woof!" said Hugo, as he chased the ball. "This is so much fun!" he barked as he wagged his tail and ran as fast as he could to catch it.

As well as fetching balls and sticks, Hugo loved playing with his friend Kitty. Kitty was a very lovable ginger cat and Kitty was also Hugo's best friend.

Their favorite game in the entire world was to chase each other. Hugo would run and run to chase Kitty and when he caught her, Kitty would then run and run to chase Hugo. They played this game every day and they never grew tired of it. They were best friends and they loved each other.

One day, however, there was a huge storm. Lightning struck, thunder boomed and the sky grew very dark. Hugo had been digging in the garden, looking for a bone that he had buried, when he suddenly looked up. The booming thunder and crackle of the lightning made him quiver and shake. He was a very, very friendly dog but he was very, very scared of storms. He ran into the bushes and hid. He didn't know what else to do!

As Hugo peered out from behind the bush where he was hiding, he could see the rain pouring down. And before long, he was very, very wet and very, very cold and very, very miserable.

The sound of the thunder hadn't stopped and he felt

alone and scared. He didn't dare leave his hiding spot. That was way too scary. But being alone in the bushes during a bad storm was even scarier still. He stood there unable to move.

Meanwhile, his friend Kitty had been sound asleep in her favorite spot on the sofa inside the house where they lived. This was the place where Kitty loved to snuggle up, especially on miserable wet days. She hadn't noticed the lightning. She hadn't noticed the thunder and she hadn't noticed the very, heavy rain that was pouring down outside.

But then a particularly loud thunder strike suddenly woke her.

"Meow!" she said as she stretched her paws and stood up slowly. "What was that loud noise?" And she wandered over to the window to peer outside into the darkness.

Just then, a flash of lightning struck and the sky lit up very brightly. In fact it was so bright that the whole backyard was aglow. It was almost as if it were daylight. But in that very moment, Kitty spotted a pale shape that seemed to be hidden amongst the bushes across the yard.

"What was that?" she wondered to herself, and peered more closely out the window hoping for a better look. Almost like magic, the sky lit up once more and this time she could clearly see the outline of her friend Hugo, shivering and shaking as he tried to hide from the storm.

Kitty new instantly, that he would be very scared. Hugo was her best friend and she knew that the thing he was most afraid of was bad storms, especially when there was thunder and lightning.

She knew that she would have to help him. The problem was, she wasn't sure how she could possibly manage it. The rain was pouring down so heavily, that the yard would surely soon flood. And then Hugo really would be in trouble. She had to do something.

So very bravely, she raced through the warm house, out the back door and faced the cold, wet darkness.

Now everyone knows that cats are not very fond of water. And Kitty was no exception. But she had no choice. She would have to go into the pouring rain to save her friend. It was up to her to be brave. Poor Hugo needed her and that's what friends are for.

Kitty took a deep breath and ventured out onto the cold, wet, muddy grass that she knew would soon be flooded. And as quickly as she could, raced across the lawn to the bush where Hugo was trying to remain hidden from the storm.

"Hugo!" she called out bravely. "It's me, Kitty! Come on! Follow me and I'll take you to safety," she yelled loudly. "You must come now or the yard may flood and no one will be able to save you!"

As soon as Hugo saw Kitty, he breathed a huge sigh

of relief. His friend had come to rescue him. He knew that he would feel safe now that she was there and very slowly edged himself out from within the dripping wet bushes.

"I'm so scared!" he called to Kitty as another loud burst of thunder roared.

"You will be ok, Hugo!" Kitty called. "Just follow me!"

And with great hesitation, Hugo stepped out from the bushes and followed Kitty across the sodden lawn that was quickly filling with water, until they had finally made it to the safety of the house.

"You saved me, Kitty!" Hugo exclaimed. "You're the bravest cat in the whole world," he said. "And you're *my* best friend!"

"You're the friendliest dog that ever was," replied Kitty. "And you're *my* best friend!"

"Well, I guess that's what friends are for," thought Hugo as he snuggled up next to Kitty in front of the fireplace later that night. And with that, the very, very friendly dog and the very, very brave cat closed their eyes and fell into a deep and peaceful sleep, both grateful to have each other as such wonderful best friends.

I hope that you and your child enjoyed reading this book.

If you can spare a few moments, I would really appreciate a review.

Thank you very much!

Katrina

Here is another book that I'm sure you and your child will also enjoy reading...

My Dragon is Scared

And here are some early reading books to set your child on the path to becoming a great reader…

CPSIA information can be obtained
at www.ICGtesting.com
Printed in the USA
LVOW04s1016110516

487737LV00022B/208/P

9 781530 959891